BOVILLE

BOVILLE

THE REGENCY
PUBLISHERS

Copyright © 2023 by Judith Mitchell.

All rights reserved. No part of this book may be reproduced in any form or by any electronic or mechanical means, including information storage and retrieval systems, without permission in writing from the author and publisher, except by reviewers, who may quote brief passages in a review.

Library of Congress Control Number: 2022920062

ISBN: 978-1-959434-88-7 (Paperback Edition)
ISBN: 978-1-959434-89-4 (Hardcover Edition)
ISBN: 978-1-959434-87-0 (E-book Edition)

Some characters and events in this book are fictitious. Any similarity to the real persons, living or dead, is coincidental and not intended by the author.

Book Ordering Information

The Regency Publishers, US
521 5th Ave 17th floor NY, NY10175
Phone Number: (315)537-3088 ext 1007
Email: info@theregencypublishers.com
www.theregencypublishers.com

Printed in the United States of America

Book Review

"The writer uses the reader's mind to play and think around the circles. Applause for the words that are easy to understand, It's the choice of words that amazes us, and convinces us that it's the kind of adventure that we, like Alma, would go on."

Sophie Jones

Book Reviewer, The Regency Publishers

DEDICATION

"To the late Michael Mason, in appreciation of our long friendship and with gratitude for his inspiration, which fostered this book".

ACKNOWLEDGMENT

"The help given to me by everyone at the Regency has been greatly appreciated; each person with whom I spoke was kind, gracious, and professional. Special thanks are due to Molly Parker, who was unfailingly supportive, encouraging, and friendly, and who opened more doors for me than I could have imagined were available. BOVILLE, Alma, Oyster, and I will be forever grateful."

BOVILLE

At a time and place far distant from our own, there lived a girl named Alma, in a small village called Boville.

Boville didn't seem unusual to Alma – it was just 'home' and was quite ordinary, and even quite boring at times. After all, she had been born there, and had lived in Boville for all her eleven years. She was used to it.

However, travelers from other places who passed through Boville thought it was damp, dark, and chilly. Few stayed long. Their good humors soon turned sour. Most travelers left Boville with an unpleasant tale or two about the surly innkeeper, the impudence of the waiter, or the rudeness of most of the merchants and officials – including the grouchy baker's wife and even Her Honor the Mayor. Unfortunately, there was a good deal of truth to these gripes and grumbles.

Even the most patient, cheerful visitors realized that their own growing bad moods were caused by more than just the terrible manners of the citizens of Boville. After leaving Boville's slippery cobblestones and getting on their way to other destinations, they would soon see sunlight brightening the road before them. And looking up, they smiled at the clear blue sky above them. When they recalled the wretched weather in

Boville it would occur to them that it had rained during their entire visit there. And if they had been to Boville more than once they would realize that in truth, it always rained there.

They were correct! Low clouds constantly hung over the village. Chilly mists drifted through the lanes and drizzle blew into everyone's eyes. Sometimes rain fell heavily and was driven by sharp winds; sometimes lighter showers drenched peoples' clothes and soaked their shoes; but damp it was – always. Unpleasant!

Travelers who had to remain a night or two stayed at Boville's one inn, The Sodden Gull. The inn stood on the square in the center of town, directly across from the grey stone house where Alma lived. On days when it merely sprinkled between downpours, Alma would look out her window and watch people arriving or departing with their dripping satchels, slipping and sliding on the mossy steps at the inn's door. But often the fog was so thick that she could see practically nothing at all.

However, at other times when the fog parted a bit it was possible to see beyond Boville's rooftops. Looming close over the chimneys rose steep cliffs which formed a mountain that encircled Boville on three sides; only the north lay open and from there, cold northerly winds blustered in and whirled through the village. This mountain was so high that only shadowy light reached the streets; even windows high up like Alma's let in such dim daylight that peoples' lamps were lit throughout the day. The sun was never seen.

Every night, moist clouds gathered from all the wide lands outside Boville and formed mist which drifted up the mountain, and in the morning all of it rolled down heavily over the village and stayed there. Almost everyone preferred staying indoors, the nearer their hearthfires the better. People were too glum to pack up and leave. They cursed the mountain, calling it "The Hateful Sleeper," and they blamed it for their miserable climate, and they wasted little time looking out the windows at it. Even Alma's family, whom she loved dearly, seldom smiled or told jokes, and they really weren't the least bit cheerful.

Alma, however – an imaginative girl who was often chided for being impractical – spent a great deal of time looking out the window. She and her cat Oyster sat close together, enjoying themselves by looking down at the village below. Alma wondered about the guests at The Sodden Gull: where were they from? And what it was like there? Oyster liked watching certain wet dogs and wondered what they were sniffing.

Sometimes on slightly clear days Alma gazed up past the farthest chimneys of Boville and studied The Hateful Sleeper. Unlike her family and the other citizens of Boville, she found this mountain very interesting and well worth watching. She was most curious about one enormous boulder which towered way up at the summit. It was the highest point on the mountaintop and it loomed up opposite her window. Everyone in the village particularly hated this oddly-shaped stone, which looked to them a bit like the heavy head of a tired old man; an old man who, they said, had no business being there. Thus the entire mountain had borne the name "Hateful Sleeper" for so long that no one could remember if it had ever had a nicer name. It was indeed an unfortunate mountain because it rose so high and spread so wide that it completely blocked the sun, and without the sun, Boville remained forever dreary.

Alma was almost the only person who really looked carefully at this craggy rock at the mountain's top. Something about it was fascinating. Although she couldn't be sure of this, it seemed to appear slightly different at different times. Wisps of fog caught in shrubs and branches at its crest could look like soft white hair. At other times rain-water streamed down cracks in the rocks like tears running down ancient cheeks, and moisture dripped from the tip of a pointed stone which stuck out like a gigantic runny nose.

If Alma turned away for a moment and then looked back again, the entire rock might appear out of the mist and then she could make out sloping stones under it which looked rather like shoulders. But a blink of an eye later, all that could be seen was a vague outline of the entire mountain. The view shifted and changed so often that Alma found it hard to recall the exactly how the rocks looked from one moment to the next. It was easy to imagine that some tiny crack was now slightly more tilted; some cranny a bit more open – perhaps more to the right – or the left? It was mysterious.

There was one other person who seemed to share Alma's interest in the mountain. At the very northern edge of the village stood a small, mildewed cottage. It well-hidden, wedged into a cranny at the bottom of the steepest cliff and it was quite apart from Boville's sturdier houses. Here lived an old, old, woman named Zephira. No one knew or cared where she had come from or how long she had lived there. Nobody paid attention to her, because they thought she was a little odd. The good citizens of Boville didn't speak to her except to buy the mushrooms she grew or the cures and potions she brewed. Certainly no one ever came by just to pay her a visit, except for Alma. Zephira was never grumpy or ill-tempered, and Alma enjoyed her company very much.

Zephira was quiet kind and patient, and listened with smiles and wise nods of her head while Alma talked. When there was a pause, Zephira would wait a bit and then she would start telling some wonderful story.

"Things were not always as they are now," she would begin in her creaky old voice. "There once was a time when…." Alma heard many stories as she sat by the warm hearth.

Sometimes Zephira talked of dragons, enchantments, and magic; sometimes Zephira told tales about a beautiful Wisewoman who once loved and lost a sad, wandering giant. And sometimes she had stories to tell of people who had long, long ago lived in Boville.

One afternoon Alma described white vapors she had watched drifting out of a hollow place near the top of the face of the Hateful Sleeper. She was excited about this, because on this morning, the cave had looked like an open mouth, and she imagined that this mist could be breath! Zephira sighed and stirred the fire so hard that bright orange flames suddenly exploded up the chimney with a whoosh.

Settling back in her chair, Zephira looked carefully at her guest and smiled a secret wise smile. She began a story, in her usual way:

"Things were not always as they are now…" her old eyes glittered in the firelight, and the fire snapped loudly. "Once our own village of Boville lay warm in the sunlight. Upon every window–sill and balcony stood pots and pots of beautiful flowers…red, and pink, and golden yellow…in the square near the inn flowed a sparkling fountain…"

This was not a familiar story at all; not another adventure of Aldis and His Floating Umbrella, nor more about Little Letha Who Almost Drowned in the Well – nor any of the tales about spells or fantastic beasts which Zephira usually told.

Zephira continued softly, "Yes…once indeed there was a time when things here were not as you see them now," she mused, and she described a Boville of some long-ago time; way before the antics of Aldis or Little Letha before him…

In that far-off time, the square in the middle of town, right in front of Alma's own house, had been surrounded by tall, shady, trees. Songbirds nested among their leaves and filled the air with the sweetest music. Breezes carried fragrances from everyone's bright and blooming gardens, blending them with delectable aromas from the bakery. The children of Boville chased and tumbled all around – without boots and raincoats! Old folks smiled at them, as they sat in the warm sunlight playing chess or whist, or other long-forgotten games. Could Boville ever have been so beautiful? Alma wondered, but she had to ask what a fountain was; what balconies were used for.

"Why did everything change so much?" She asked next.

Zephira did not answer right away. Instead, she rose and hobbled over to her small window and looked up at the mountain, rising there so close against her cottage. A sheet of rain rattled suddenly rattled the windowpanes. At that, Zephira gave another great sigh and for just a moment the air cleared and mossy rocks were visible. The old woman turned back and smiled at Alma, and she made the strangest suggestion:

"Why don't you ask the Hateful Sleeper?" Zephira asked, and passed slowly back through the room, past the fire where Alma sat, and down the steps into her dark pantry "…way up at the top…" she murmured softly, "…ask him yourself…." Her voice faded away, and although Alma could faintly hear her moving about –rearranging things – Zephira did not reappear.

Alma was puzzled, and sat and thought and thought. Ask the Hateful Sleeper? Talk to a *mountain?* And ask it what? Up at the top? Wouldn't this mean climbing the mountain? But that was forbidden! No one had ever climbed up the mountain – no one was permitted to, and at any rate, why on earth would the good citizens of Boville want to do such a foolish thing? The rocks were wet and cold, the dark cliffs were perilously steep and always so foggy that it would be impossible for a person see ahead of themselves more than a foot or two. Then there would be the same miserable stones at the top. Such a treacherous climb would be completely pointless; that was the end of it. In fact, all Boville's children were sternly warned against even going near the fallen rocks at its feet. None of them was even interested. Her brothers and sisters found the mountain very boring and her parents frowned upon Alma's interest in it.

Suddenly, Alma jumped up! She took a deep breath. To climb the Hateful Sleeper – what an exciting adventure! All the stories that Zephira had told her were of great adventures – wasn't it about time for her to have one, too? She called goodbye and thank you, and she and Oyster splashed home in a great hurry.

Unfortunately, the rest of the day was especially dreary, so her hopes of plotting a pathway up to the mountaintop from her seat at the window were in vain. She had to sit impatiently there next to Oyster, waiting for the fog to lift, which it did not.

Plan or no plan, before dawn the next morning as Boville still lay blanketed in darkness and mist, Alma pulled on her sturdiest boots, buckled up her thickest raincoat, and called Oyster. She was certain that Oyster had explored the cliffs and knew some clever trails leading at least part–way to the top. "If I just follow him I'll be able to climb up quite easily," she declared.

The two of them slipped quietly through the gloom, arriving at the bottom of the mountain opposite her own home at a place hidden behind the other houses. Alma didn't want anyone to notice them climbing, someone who might summon the whole village to demand that they come back down and then punish them for trying.

"This is the perfect spot for us to begin our adventure!" she whispered to Oyster. Oyster, being a cat and curious about what his mistress was hunting, was quite agreeable.

Alas; when Alma looked upwards, she saw nothing but whiteness. No sign of the mountain could she see; in fact, when she stretched out her hands she could see little of anything beyond her fingertips. What if the mountain – The Hateful Sleeper himself -- was hiding on purpose this day? And now Oyster himself was nowhere to be seen. Had he headed back to his warm cushion at home? She paused in dismay.

She was about to turn away in discouragement when she heard a familiar "meow" somewhere above her. As she had hoped, Oyster was leading her up to the top! She reached out and grasped a slimy handhold, found a crack to fit her boot in, and began hauling herself up the rocks. It was easy enough, at first.

Alma realized soon after her brave start – maybe ten feet up – that the villagers might have been right. This was indeed treacherous. It was awfully slippery and awfully steep. Safe footholds were few; good handholds took minutes to find. Wet moss tore off under her fingers; her boots slid on dangerously loose stones; and where the invisible Oyster was, somewhere above her, she could not tell. She clung, trembling, to small cracks and crevasses and groped for the next ones, hoping they would support her. Worst of all, Alma realized miserably that she could not turn back. Never would she be able to retrace her way back down without falling. She could only continue this frightening climb upwards; she had dared to take a chance – and now, it had taken her.

And it dawned on her suddenly that she had been so excited about having an adventure that she had not given a single thought to what questions to ask the Hateful Sleeper! Wasn't that why was she here? Alma's hands were wet and freezing; she felt very small and very stupid, and she wanted to cry.

However, she struggled slowly up inch by terrifying inch, because there didn't seem to be anything else to do. Finally after what seemed like hours, she found she was approaching the source of Oyster's meowing, which grew louder as she climbed. Oyster had reached a flat place above her and he waited for Alma, calling to guide her. At last she pulled herself up onto the ledge and flopped down, panting, gasping, and shaking, to rest next to her purring cat.

But – where were they? After catching her breath, Alma looked around. Stretching along the right and left sides of the flat rock on which she and Oyster sat, lay long, oddly-twisted ridges of stone. She stared at them and recognized them as some peculiar rocks that stood a little way below the mountaintop – she had studied them from her window way down in Boville. She gasped! These were the rocks which she had pretended were long fingers with gnarled knuckles. How strange it was that now, up close, they looked even more like old fingers!

Alma looked higher up. It was all as she had imagined it might be, so many times while she sat in her room so far below. Right here, hanging over her head, was the familiar massive outcropping of rock bristling with roots and twigs – it was as if she was sitting right under that enormous stubbly chin.

"Ha-HA!" cried Alma to Oyster, "Here we are, right under the Hateful Sleeper's chin! I've really climbed the whole way up to the top!" Far below them slept unhappy Boville, forever wrapped in a blanket of fog and rain, still dreaming in the dark despite the coming dawn.

She thought proudly, "This is the hardest thing that I have ever done in my whole entire life."

Alma got to her feet and walked along between the fingers to the front edge of the rock. Big drops of water fell on her face, splashing down from the pointed stone that jutted out overhead – it was that huge rocky "nose." How even more like an old man's nose it looked to her here, when she was so much nearer! She tilted her head back and could dimly make out a long, narrow crack above it, was it an eye?

"This really is the Sleeper himself!" Alma cried in amazement. Her voice sounded loud and echo-y, even though it was muffled by thick white mist. Oyster yowled noisily in agreement. Then…did the rock under them move just a little?

From somewhere far above, a small clod of earth dislodged and fell at her feet. A tiny green plant grew from it. Alma picked up the clump of dirt and looked at it curiously; in Boville, nothing grew except moss and fungi. Completely forgetting why she was there, she thought, "I'm going to climb even higher! I might find some more interesting plants like this…"

But all had become dimmer and foggier. "This is getting very annoying!" declared Alma, and then she saw where the mist was coming from. Just as she had described it to Zephira – ribbons of white vapor were floating out of that cave above her; from out of the big hole in the rock above the chin and under the nose…heavy mist, drifting down and landing on Oyster and her, from… she squinted and wiped the moisture out of her eyes…right out of the Hateful Sleeper's mouth! "Oh, UCK! All this horrible clammy fog, day in, day out, year after year after *year!*" she muttered crossly. A big gust of chilly whiteness blew across her upturned face and Alma began to shiver. Suddenly she was very tired of mist and fog, and she felt very cold and wet, and she grew very, very angry. And then, questions burst out of her without her even thinking.

"Hey, you! Sleeper! *Sleeper!*" Alma yelled furiously, as loud as she could, "Why do you blow fog at us?" She stamped her feet and Oyster gave an earsplitting yowl and more clumps of earth tumbled down around them. She shouted, "Why do you cover Boville with your cold breath? Why did you hide the sun?"

Then, as the massive stone face above her vanished behind the mist again, Alma took a deep breath. And why she did this she would never know. Alma blew and blew all her breath back up at the Sleeper's face, as hard as she could! Again and again with all her strength, and even as she grew very dizzy and faint, she blew and blew and blew!

All of a sudden the boulders around where she stood began to teeter and quake. Great rumbling, cracking sounds filled the air. Then with a terrifying shudder the whole mountain began to heave this way and that – Alma crouched down and held Oyster tightly and shut her eyes – and they felt a tremendous wind whirl about them, like a gigantic yawn. They heard thunderous crashes and groans and they were spun off their feet and paws and turned round and round by the roaring wind.

The wind lifted them up and spun them, spiraling higher and higher – far above the crumbling, tumbling, mountain -- they seemed to fly about forever!

Some time later, Alma opened her eyes. Oyster was lying on her stomach, licking a scratch on her cheek. They both rested upon a mound of soft earth, right in the middle of Boville's square. People stood in a circle around them, gaping with wonder and smiling with delight. Alma opened her eyes wider and wider, and raised her hand to shield them from a bright light all around her – her hand was dry! Her hand made a shadow on the earth under it! She sat up and stared around and saw that everyone had a shadow. The sun was shining down on Boville!

No one could explain this. No one could understand it. What sensible questions could they ask and to whom should they ask them? At first, it was hard to believe that the Hateful Sleeper no longer lay around their town…. that the enormous mountain had completely disappeared without a trace. It was almost as if, some said with a laugh, the old fellow had been awakened, shaken himself off, and walked away! But after a week or so of puzzlement, nobody cared any longer because they all spent every day strolling through the dry streets of their pretty little town, cheerfully greeting their fine neighbors, telling jokes, and laughing together. In the evenings they sang lovely songs and danced around a fountain in the middle of the square.

Judith Mitchell

They marveled at all the beautiful plants and flowers that had miraculously sprung from all the earth which had rained down upon Boville on that strange day. A very welcome rain this one was, for a change!

Since no one knew, and no one knows even to this day, that an impractical, imaginative girl had dared climb up and boldly ask questions of a mountain, not a single person thought to question Alma. In any event, what could Alma have told them? Would anyone have believed her story?

Sadly, no one but Alma missed the odd old woman Zephira. No one but Alma would wonder where she had gone, and with whom; but then again – no one but Alma had been told Zephira's tales of a beautiful wisewoman, who long ago had loved a wandering giant…..

****

In telling stories to the many, many children of Beauville who came to visit her over many, many years, Alma told and retold all the old tales that Zephira had told her when Alma was a little girl herself. She also told them stories of a brilliant cat named Oyster, and about Oyster and herself peering up through mist at a mysterious, bothersome mountain, in a village below it, soaked with rain. The children listened and laughed and could not imagine what that would have been like, and skipped off for a while to play among Alma's flowers, running like warm breezes through the poppies and foxgloves.

Then when they came back inside from the sunlit garden they would beg to hear again about the time long ago, when a young girl had taken a strange suggestion from an old wisewoman, and they all listened spellbound to that tale of great adventure – the difficult climb made by such a courageous girl and her curious, loyal, fearless cat, long ago, to ask some very important questions.

"Things were not always as you find them today…" Alma would begin, "There was once a time when…" and Alma would describe the Boville of her own childhood, before it was called Beauville.

Some of the children asked her questions about the Hateful Sleeper; if they asked too many whys and hows – as imaginative children will do – Alma would not answer. She would smile and nod her old head wisely, and sit quietly. Maybe she knew the answers and possibly she did not. Maybe there were no answers. Some of the children might someday find and face their own Hateful Sleepers, and climb, each one, on their own, as it must be.

www.ingramcontent.com/pod-product-compliance
Lightning Source LLC
LaVergne TN
LVHW050138080526
838202LV00061B/6526